Goose and Cloud

This book belongs to:

_____

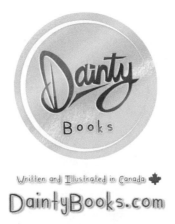

Written and Illustrated in Canada 🍁
DaintyBooks.com

ISBN # 978-1-7773479-2-5

Written By: Candace Carrothers

Illustrated By: Adrienne Brown

Produced By: Jennifer Dainty

Special thanks to these cool kids:
Lauren, Ember, Kara and Trevor

The End.

Follow Goose and Cloud
on their next adventure.

Made in the USA
Las Vegas, NV
30 November 2024

12846008R00021